for James and Helen

Henry Holt and Company, LLC, *Publishers since 1866*
115 West 18th Street, New York, New York 10011

Henry Holt is a registered trademark of Henry Holt and Company, LLC

First published in the United States in 2000 by Henry Holt and Company, LLC
Published in Canada by Fitzhenry & Whiteside Ltd.,
195 Allstate Parkway, Markham, Ontario L3R 4T8.
Originally published in the United Kingdom in 1999 by Andersen Press Ltd.

Library of Congress Cataloging-in-Publication Data
Brown, Ruth.
Holly: the true story of a cat / Ruth Brown.
Summary: Abandoned as a kitten, a cat is taken in by a family at Christmas
and becomes an important part of the household.
[1. Cats—Fiction.]   I. Title.
PZ7.B81698Ho   2000   [E]—dc21   99-59561

ISBN 0-8050-6500-8 / First American Edition—2000
The artist used acrylic paints, Doctor Martin's concentrated watercolors,
and charcoal pencil to create the illustrations for this book.
Printed in Italy
1 3 5 7 9 10 8 6 4 2

HOLLY

❧ The True Story of a Cat ❧

· RUTH BROWN ·

HENRY HOLT AND COMPANY · NEW YORK

She was just a tiny kitten and she was abandoned.

Someone found her

and gave her to us.

Because it was nearly Christmas,

we called her Holly.

She was timid at first,

but as she grew she became more relaxed.

Gradually she got used to us

and settled into her new home.

As she became more confident,

she spent long, happy days exploring her new world.

But sometimes she would sit quite still,

thinking deep thoughts.

When she was completely grown,

she had two kittens of her own.

Sometimes Holly tried to sneak away
for some peace and quiet.

But Buddy and Baby usually found her.

Holly is older now but she's still the boss.

And she is still quick enough to catch me "presents."

Holly often turns her back on the world
and ignores everybody.

Yet, every afternoon when I am working,
she keeps me company.

Our house would seem very empty without her—

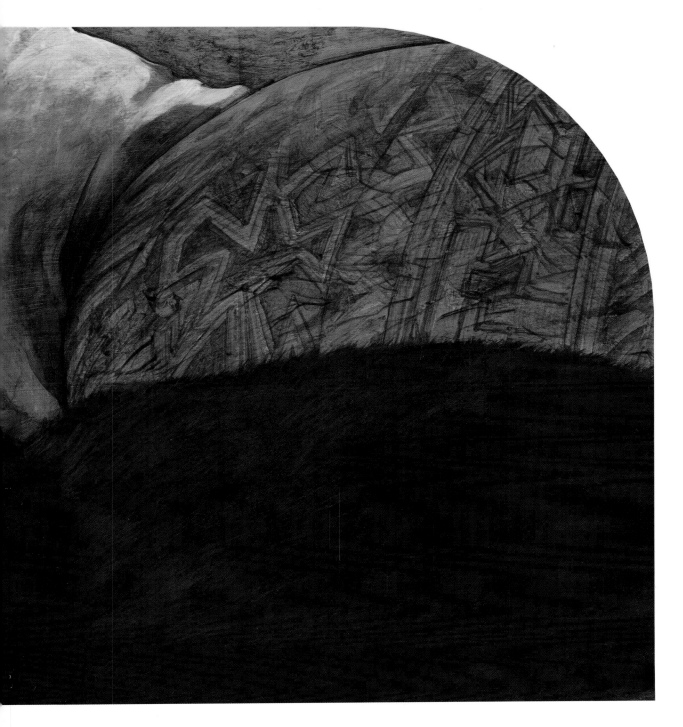

our big, beautiful, beloved Holly.